MERRY CHRISTMAS, LITTLE CRITTER!

BY MERCER MAYER

To Niko Sansevere

HarperFestival®

A Division of HarperCollins Publishers

Library of Congress catalog card number: 2003115867
A Big Tuna Trading Company, LLC/J. R. Sansevere Book
www.harperchildrens.com   www.littlecritter.com
14 15 16 SCP 20 19 18 17 16 15 14
❖
First Edition

Every Christmas, Little Sister and
I write our letters to Santa.

Then we mail them all
the way to the North Pole.

We go sledding at Grandma and Grandpa's farm. I pull the sled up, up, up . . .

. . . then we go
down faster and
faster and faster!

We all decorate the house for
Christmas. Mom and Little Sister
hang the wreath.

"Don't worry, Dad,
I'll untangle you."

I help Dad string the lights around and around the Christmas tree.

Dad and I go Christmas shopping.

I find the perfect gift for Mom.

We sing Christmas carols around the neighborhood.

Yum! Yum! "Thanks for the eggnog!"

On Christmas eve, I go to bed,
but I can't sleep. Suddenly, I hear
a sound on the roof.

I run to
the window.

On Christmas
morning, we open
all of our gifts.

Finally, there is just one
gift left under the tree. It is
the biggest gift of all.

"Wow! Thank you, Santa!"

It says, MERRY CHRISTMAS, LITTLE CRITTER! LOVE, SANTA